D1318053

World of Reading

LEVEL 1

STAR WARS REBELS™

ZEB
TO THE RESCUE

ADAPTED BY MICHAEL SIGLAIN

BASED ON THE EPISODE "ENTANGLEMENT,"
WRITTEN BY HENRY GILROY AND SIMON KINBERG

ABDO
Spotlight

Disney • LUCASFILM
PRESS

Los Angeles • New York

ABDOPUBLISHING.COM

Reinforced library bound edition published in 2018 by Spotlight, a division of ABDO,
PO Box 398166, Minneapolis, Minnesota 55439. Spotlight produces high-quality
reinforced library bound editions for schools and libraries. Published by
Disney • Lucasfilm Press, an imprint of Disney Book Group.

Printed in the United States of America, North Mankato, Minnesota.
042017
092017

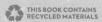
THIS BOOK CONTAINS
RECYCLED MATERIALS

LIBRARY OF CONGRESS CATALOGING-IN-PUBLICATION DATA

This title was previously cataloged with the following information:

Siglain, Michael.
 Zeb to the rescue / adapted by Michael Siglain.
  p. cm. -- (World of reading. Level 1)
Summary: Zeb, a member of the rebel group, battles Storm Troopers to help an old
man and his droid.
1. Extraterrestrial beings--Juvenile fiction. 2. Space warfare--Juvenile fiction. 3.
Adventure stories. 4. Extraterrestrial beings--Fiction. 5. Space warfare--Fiction. 6.
Adventure and adventurers--Fiction. 7. Adventure stories. 8. Extraterrestrial beings.
9. Space warfare.
PZ7.S57754 Ze 2014
[E]--dc23
                    2014937081

978-1-5321-4056-3 (Reinforced Library Bound Edition)

Spotlight
A Division of ABDO
abdopublishing.com

Meet Zeb.

Zeb is big
and strong.

Zeb is a rebel.

He fights for what is right.

One day, on the
planet Lothal,
Zeb got into a fight.

Zeb was supposed to
meet his friend.

They were supposed
to meet in an alley.

But Zeb was in
the wrong alley.

Zeb saw a man and a droid.
They were in trouble.

Troopers were
stealing from them.

This made Zeb mad.
Zeb wanted to help.

Zeb used his strength.

He knocked their
heads together.

Zeb saved the man
and the droid.

Then more troopers
joined the fight.

The troopers
chased Zeb.

They could not
find Zeb.

So Zeb found them.

Zeb used his bo-rifle to stun
the troopers.

Even more troopers
joined the fight.
Zeb hid on top of a ship.

He surprised the troopers.

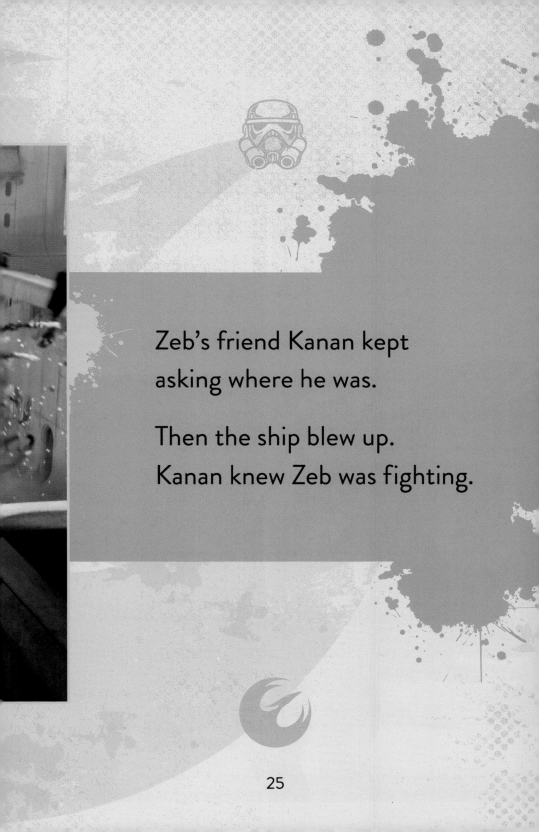

Zeb's friend Kanan kept
asking where he was.

Then the ship blew up.
Kanan knew Zeb was fighting.

The troopers
were no match
for Zeb.

The man and the droid
went to find Zeb.

The man and the droid
found Zeb in an alley.
They wanted to thank him.

They offered Zeb money.

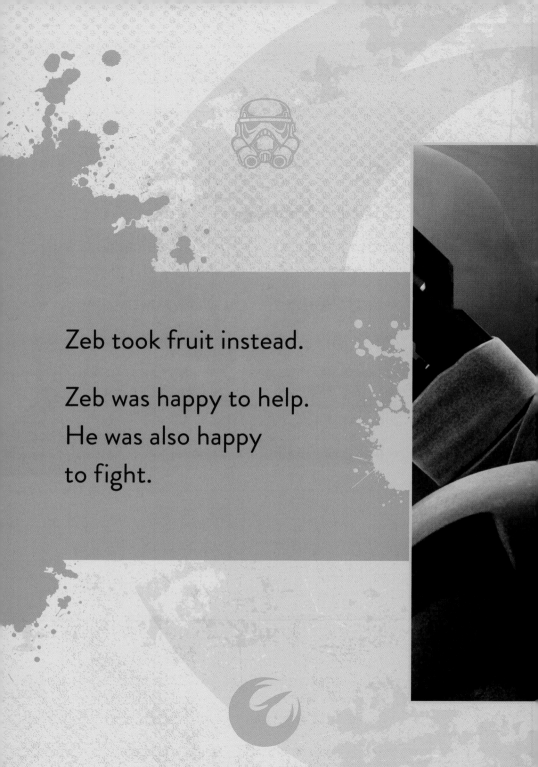

Zeb took fruit instead.

Zeb was happy to help.
He was also happy
to fight.

Zeb likes to stand up
for what is right.
Zeb is a rebel.